My Two Grandmothers

EFFIN OLDER

Illustrated by NANCY HAYASHI

Harcourt, Inc.

San Diego   New York   London

Requests for permission to make copies of any part of the work should be mailed to
the following address: Permissions Department, Harcourt, Inc.,
6277 Sea Harbor Drive, Orlando, Florida 32887-6777.

www.harcourt.com

Library of Congress Cataloging-in-Publication Data
Older, Effin.
My two grandmothers/Effin Older; illustrated by Nancy Hayashi.
p. cm.
Summary: After Lily celebrates Hanukkah with one of her grandmothers
and Christmas with the other, she plans a special party for both of them.
[1. Grandmothers—Fiction. 2. Parties—Fiction. 3. Hanukkah—Fiction.
4. Christmas—Fiction.] I. Hayashi, Nancy, ill. II. Title.
PZ7.O45344My 2000
[E]—dc21   99-6092
ISBN 0-15-200785-7

First edition

H G F E D C B A

Printed in Singapore

*The illustrations in this book were done in watercolor and
Prismacolor pencil on hot press Arches watercolor paper.
The display type was set in Ribbon.
The text type was set in Perpetua.
Printed and bound by Tien Wah Press, Singapore
This book was printed on totally chlorine-free Nymolla Matte Art paper.
Production supervision by Ginger Boyer
Designed by Judythe Sieck*

For my mother, Phyllis Lawes,
and my mother-in-law, Ruth Older—
two special grandmothers —E. O.

To Anita, Laura, Lisze, Marla, Mary Ann,
and Naomi, with appreciation —N. H.

$\mathscr{I}$ have two grandmothers, Grammy Lane and Bubbe Silver.

Grammy Lane lives on a farm and wears aprons with pretty little flowers.

Bubbe Silver lives in a tall apartment building and wears big red glasses with a fancy gold chain.

Grammy and Bubbe live so far apart,
I have to take turns visiting them.
Every summer I go to Grammy Lane's
farm. She takes me for rides on the tractor
and lets *me* steer.

After I visit the farm, I go to stay with Bubbe in her apartment. She takes me to play golf and lets *me* hit the ball. Hitting the ball is fun, but the best part of golf is lunch in the clubhouse.

"Please bring me and my *mamaleh* a Donald Duck," Bubbe says, and the waiter brings us each a magic drink with red on the bottom, blue in the middle, and green on the top.

It's magic because the red never mixes with the blue and the blue never mixes with the green.

Once I said to Bubbe, "My name is Lily. Why do you call me Mamaleh?"

Bubbe pulled me onto her lap. "*Mamaleh* means little mother. That's what *my* Bubbe called me. It's a Silver tradition."

Bubbe says she's a snowbird. That means when she sees the first snowflake, she gets on a jet and flies to her other apartment—the one on the beach. Bubbe says snow is for polar bears.

I say snow is for having fun. So does
Grammy Lane.
Grammy has two pairs of snowshoes in
her attic—a big pair for her and a little pair
for me.

We look for animal tracks in the snow. Grammy whispers, "If we're real quiet, we might spot a rabbit."

When our toes get cold, Grammy says, "Come on, Pumpkin. It's time for some red flannel hash to warm up our insides."

"*Flannel?* Like my pajamas?"

Grammy laughs. "Heavens, no! *Flannel* because it warms you up. My mother, your great-grandmother, taught me how to make it. I'll teach you someday, too. It's a Lane tradition."

The next time I see Bubbe, it's Hanukkah.
I tell her about Grammy's red flannel hash.

"Sounds like my gefilte fish," says Bubbe.
"My mother, your great-grandmother, taught
me how to make it. It's a Silver tradition."

"Will you teach me?" I ask.

Bubbe hugs me. "But of course!"

I love Bubbe's gefilte fish. I take a big bite loaded with extra hot horseradish.

Suddenly fireworks explode in my nose. Tears roll down my cheeks.

Bubbe laughs. "So how's the horseradish, Mamaleh?"

I can't answer. The horseradish has stolen my breath.

On the first night of Hanukkah, Bubbe and
I set the menorah on a special white tablecloth.
We put one candle in the middle and one candle
on the end.

Then we make latkes. Stacks of latkes.
We Silvers *love* latkes!

Pretty soon Bubbe's apartment is filled
with aunts and uncles and cousins. Everyone
holds hands around the menorah. Bubbe
lights the Hanukkah candles, and we sing
a prayer in Hebrew.

After the prayer, the kids get presents.
Then we all eat latkes. Sometimes I eat so
many, my stomach feels like it's going to burst.

Right after Hanukkah at Bubbe's, I go to Grammy's for Christmas. Hurray! Two holidays in a row!

On Christmas morning, we open presents.

I rip off the paper to see what's inside. Grammy unwraps each present very carefully, so she can use the bows and paper again next Christmas.

When all the presents have been opened,
I play games with my cousins and eat Grammy's
chocolate fudge until it's time for dinner.

Christmas dinner looks just like a
picture in a book: turkey with stuffing,
mashed potatoes, cranberry sauce, and
Grammy's warm homemade rolls.
　　And for dessert? Pie. Apple, raspberry,
pumpkin, and mince. We Lanes *love* pie!

After dinner we gather around Grammy's old piano to sing Christmas carols. My favorite is "Away in a Manger."

When Christmas is over, I think about my two grandmothers. I think about how Grammy Lane never gets to light Hanukkah candles or sip a Donald Duck drink. I think about how Bubbe Silver never gets to sing Christmas carols or look for animal tracks in the snow.

Then I get an idea.

I take out my stationery with the little green frogs hopping along the top. I write one invitation to Bubbe and another one to Grammy.

The day of my party, I blow up balloons
and paint a sign to hang over the table.
I make three reddy-bluey-greeny Donald
Duck drinks. The colors kind of run together.
Then I wait for my two grandmothers.

Bubbe arrives from the city and Grammy arrives from the farm. They each have a box.

Bubbe asks, "So where's the party, Mamaleh? I don't see any party hats."

Grammy asks, "Have we come on the wrong day, Pumpkin? Where's the cake and ice cream?"

"Look!" I point to my sign.

"You mean it's a party just for us?" asks Grammy.

"Just grandmothers?" asks Bubbe.

"Yes! Just grandmothers. It's a new tradition."

My grandmothers smile at each other.

"She's just like a Silver," says Bubbe to Grammy.

"Every inch a Lane," says Grammy to Bubbe.

I lead my two grandmothers to the party table. Grammy hands me the box she's carrying. "Here's something traditional for you, Pumpkin," she says. It's red flannel hash and an apple pie.

Bubbe hands me her box. "And here's something else traditional for you, Mamaleh." Gefilte fish and horseradish–*extra hot* horseradish!

I bring my two grandmothers
reddy-bluey-greeny Donald Duck
drinks. I give myself one, too.

"To the start of a new tradition!" I say.
Bubbe says, "A Lane-Silver tradition!"
Grammy says, "A Silver-Lane tradition!"

And then we eat.